Kelly's Creek

DORIS BUCHANAN SMITH

Kelly's Creek

Illustrated by Alan Tiegreen

Thomas Y. Crowell Company　　New York

By the Author
A Taste of Blackberries
Kick a Stone Home
Kelly's Creek

Library of Congress Cataloging in Publication Data

Smith, Doris Buchanan. Kelly's creek.
SUMMARY: A nine-year-old boy's struggle to cope with a special physical problem is relieved by daily visits to a marsh and learning about its marine life. [1. Physically handicapped—Fiction. 2. Marshes—Fiction] I. Tiegreen, Alan. II. Title. PZ7.S64474Ke
[Fic] 75-6761 ISBN 0-690-00731-0

1 2 3 4 5 6 7 8 9 10

For the men in my life:
my father, my husband, my sons.

Kelly's Creek

Chapter One

Nine-year-old Kelly O'Brien inched his way home. Folded inside one of his books was his monthly "progress report." It showed the same marks as last time.

Two houses away from home Kelly saw Zack tossing a football to himself. The ball spiraled high, then dropped to Zack's waiting arms.

"Hey, throw it to me," Kelly called, setting his books on the curb. Kelly hated ball games, but anything was better than showing the "progress report" to his mother.

"Come on, throw it," Kelly said again, holding his hands ready. In two months of special classes, since January, Kelly had shown "no progress." Progress, that is, improvement, was what his parents were demanding. Without it Kelly knew that doom was going to fall on his head.

Zack was frowning. "Catch it this time, Kelly," he shouted, drawing back and throwing the ball.

Kelly looked over his shoulder at the football as he ran. Gritting his teeth and squinting, he lunged for the ball. It fell crashing to the ground just out of the reach of his fingers. Kelly tripped over his own feet and, like Jack, went tumbling after.

"Kelly, you are hopeless," Zack groaned. He stood with his hands on his hips and glared at Kelly. Kelly grinned to cover his inside feelings.

He picked himself up and brushed off grass and dirt. Lining up behind the ball, he kicked it toward Zack. Instead of going to Zack, the ball skittered crazily and bobbed into the street.

"Oh, Kelly," Zack said loudly, running after the ball.

Kelly sighed. Having Zack disgusted with him was almost as bad as showing the progress report to his parents. Zack used to be his best friend. But since Zack and the others had learned to play ball Kelly didn't have any real friends. Except, maybe, Phillip.

Quickly he gathered up his books and darted home. It always surprised him how well he could run if it was just plain running. It was when he had to think and run at the same time that his feet got mixed up.

In the carport, he noticed with relief that his mother's car was gone. Shannon, his sister, was at the kitchen table playing cards with her friend Nancy.

"Where's Mom?" he asked. Shannon shrugged and didn't take her eyes off her cards. She could be a snob sometimes. Thirteen, Kelly had decided, must be a bad age.

"I'll be at the creek," he said, setting his books on the kitchen counter.

"Where's your progress report, Kelly?" Shannon asked in a sassy voice, still not looking up from the cards. "And you'd better do your exercises." Kelly ignored her. Who was she to tell him to do his exercises? He pushed the back door open and wandered out into the warm winter afternoon.

On the plain grass, he tripped. "Dang," he said to himself. His feet were clumsy, his hands were clumsy, and he was clumsy inside his head. The exercises were supposed to help him get over his clumsiness but they weren't helping. Exercises made him sick; he forgot them before he crossed the yard.

At the end of the backyard he climbed down a small bluff. Brunswick, where he lived, was in southeast Georgia near the Atlantic Ocean. For miles around there were marshes that were crisscrossed with tidal creeks. A runlet curved right up to the edge of Kelly's backyard. It formed a semicircle from, and back to, one of the larger creeks, called Big Marshy.

The straw-gold of the late-winter marsh matched his hair and eyes and freckles. Kelly dropped into his

4

boat as he'd done so many times before. He took a life jacket from the waterproof compartment under the seat. Almost without thinking, he buckled it around himself. Wearing the life jacket was his parents' most important rule of the creek. The next most important rule was knowing how to swim. Kelly was a good strong swimmer. He knew frog kicks and scissor kicks and every kind of swimming stroke. He was never clumsy in the water.

Slipping the rope off the hitching post, he pushed against the mud with his paddle. At low tide there was more pushing than paddling. The creek was barely boat-wide. But at high tide the water rose above all the mucky mud. At those times, sometimes the creek was fifteen feet wide.

Fiddler crabs scurried for their holes as the boat scraped past. Some merely stood, staring with their popeyes that sat on their heads like glasses.

"You know I'm your friend, don't you?" Kelly said aloud to all the tiny crabs that didn't run.

To make the creek safe for Kelly, Mr. O'Brien had fenced off the ends. The fences kept Kelly from going out into Big Marshy. Big Marshy flowed through the marsh to the river and the sea. At low tide Big Marshy wasn't much more than boat-wide itself. But when the tide came in, a shrimp boat could cruise Big Marshy.

The runlet was only for Kelly's boat. At one end Mr. O'Brien had put a wide gate. One of these days he was going to get a motorboat for the family. He planned to keep it in the runlet. Through the gate they could get into Big Marshy. In the meantime, the gate was kept locked. It was to the gate that Kelly mud-poled his way, hoping Phillip would be there.

"Phillip. Phillip?" Kelly called. Phillip was a biology student at the Brunswick Junior College and was doing a study of life in the marsh.

"Ho," came Phillip's answering cry. Just beyond the gate and to the left was an area which Phillip had staked off with sticks and string. Since they had met in the marsh a few weeks ago Phillip had taught Kelly the names of things that Kelly already knew from observance. In a minute Phillip appeared at the edge of the marsh.

The gate wobbled as Kelly flipped the boat rope over the gatepost. Dad was supposed to fix it. Stepping onto the bank, he sank halfway to his knees in mud. He laughed and didn't mind at all. It made him feel like Phillip. Phillip was mud-caked to his knees every time Kelly saw him. When Phillip came to the marsh he was always in muddy sneakers and faded, cutoff jeans. His skinny chest and legs were covered with dark curly hair, as was his head.

Happily, Kelly lifted his legs high. Curling his toes, he brought his feet up toes-first to keep his sneakers on his feet.

"What are you doing today?" Kelly asked. He stepped from the mushy creek bank to the firm but spongy marsh floor.

"Just observing and recording," Phillip said. "I have a lot more sketches to make." Phillip kept a record of his observations in a muddy notebook.

"When can I see your other notebook?" Kelly asked. He followed Phillip toward the study area. Mud from his legs dribbled into his shoes; his feet squished with each step. In the other notebook, Phillip had told him, things were written neatly and there were illustrations showing everything about the observations. Kelly admired people who could draw. He couldn't even draw a circle or a square or the letters of the alphabet, much less a fiddler crab. He had been told it was a perception problem. Something about mixed-up signals between his brain and his eyes, hands, and feet.

Phillip stooped by the string that marked off the study area. "See?" he said, picking up a fiddler crab and turning it upside-down. "Soon she will have eggs under here." Phillip lifted a small hinged flap under the tiny creature. Kelly already knew the flap was called an apron; it was for the protection of the eggs.

"What kind is it?" Phillip asked.

"A blue mud fiddler, *Uca pugnax,*" Kelly answered.

"How do you know?"

"Because of the blue dot between her eyes," Kelly said. "And she's darker than the sand fiddler so she'll match the mud."

"Good boy, Kelly," Phillip said. "I wish I had known

so much about the marsh when I was nine years old."

Kelly grinned with pleasure, and he settled into a sitting position in preparation for observing. Away from this marsh, Kelly thought, people think I'm dumb. But here, alone with Phillip and the creatures of the marsh, Phillip knew—and Kelly himself knew—that he was smart enough.

Chapter Two

The voice of one of the land people was calling him now.
"Kelly! Kelly!" It was Shannon's voice bellowing over
the silence of the marsh. Kelly scrambled to his feet and
stepped away from the marked-off area. They never
talked loudly when they were near Phillip's study area.

"Coming," he hollered, repeating it to make sure
she heard him. "That's my sister," he said to Phillip.

"Uh-oh," Phillip said.

"You know about sisters, huh?" Kelly said as he
started walking.

"Yup," Phillip grunted, pushing himself up and
trailing along behind Kelly.

As he came out of the marsh, Kelly saw Shannon
standing at the edge of the bluff, hands on hips. Her
friend Nancy was with her.

"You're late for supper," Shannon screamed. Her

mouth was round with yelling. Kelly thought an orange would probably fit into Shannon's big mouth. He grinned and waved. It was harder, he had learned, for people to be angry with a person who kept on grinning.

"Coming," he called again. Over his shoulder, he looked at Phillip and shrugged.

"I'll see you," Phillip said. Kelly nodded, and he mushed his way around the end of the fence and stepped into his boat. With one arm he unleashed the boat; with the other he raked loose marsh grass away from the gate. The loose grass pressed against the fence, and it was his job to keep the fence clear so the water would flow freely. He flipped the grass over the fence. Phillip looked back and waved before disappearing into the marsh. Kelly liked to think of the marsh grass floating out to sea. The marsh grass from this very creek, Phillip had told him, would feed fish in the deep ocean.

"You better hurry," Shannon yelled. She was showing off for Nancy. They were like a shoe and a sock, Kelly thought. And they giggled a lot, mostly about *boys*.

"You better get that mud washed off and get to the table," she continued when he had clambered up the bank. "And who was that man?"

"Oh, that's Phillip," Kelly said, looking out toward the study area. There was no sign of Phillip. "He knows everything about the marsh."

"I'll bet Mother and Daddy don't know there are weirdos wandering around the marsh."

"Phillip's not a weirdo," Kelly said. He stopped at the outside spigot while Shannon and Nancy went in, letting the door bang.

"Kelly's been talking to some awful-looking man in the marsh," Shannon's voice came back out through the door. Kelly stuck his feet and legs under the stream of water, using his hands to rub off the mud. Pulling off his sneakers, he rinsed the insides and left them on the steps.

"What's this about a man in the marsh?" Mother asked as he came in. She was pouring tea into glasses.

"It's my friend, Phillip," he answered.

"Well, hurry and change clothes. I need you to put the tea on the table. We'll talk about Phillip later." He nodded and started through the family room toward the stairway. "And take these books with you," she added. Kelly darted back and swooped up the books from the counter where he'd left them. His heart was thudding at the thought of the "no progress" report inside one of the books.

"Hi, sport," Dad said, looking up from the television. "Been playing a tough game of ball?" Kelly looked down at himself. He did look as if he'd been playing something rough. He grinned, thinking how pleased his father would be if he liked to play football.

"Yes, sir," he lied.

"Wooo-wooo," Shannon crooned accusingly, but she didn't say anything else. Dad, satisfied, was back watching the news. Kelly mounted the steps.

In the bathroom he splashed his hands and face and wiped them dry. Traces of marsh mud smeared off on the yellow towel. Kelly shoved it into the dirty clothes hamper. Slipping one shirt off over his head, he dropped it on the floor and took another from the top drawer. He pulled it on as he ran downstairs, and skidded around the corner into the kitchen.

Without stopping he grabbed two glasses of iced tea from the counter, sipping at one on the way to the table.

"Kelly," Mother scolded. "Please wait until we're all at the table."

"I'm thirsty, Mom," he said, taking another swig and setting that glass down by his own plate. His fingers had erased the frosty condensation from the glass.

"Now, what's this about a friend in the marsh?" Mother asked him. Then she looked over his head and spoke to Dad. "Shannon says there was a man in the marsh with Kelly."

"He was barefooted, had no shirt, and had the bushiest hair you ever saw," Shannon added. She squinted her eyes and wrinkled her nose.

"In the marsh?" Dad asked. "I thought you said you

were playing football." Shannon continued making faces, directing them at Kelly. Kelly put the last two glasses on the table and sat quickly. Avoiding his father's eyes, he bowed his head and waited for the blessing.

"You spend entirely too much time in that creek," Dad said as he sat down. Unfolding his napkin onto his lap, he bowed and blessed the food.

"Why don't you develop some other interests?" Dad said as though he had never stopped for the blessing. "Like sports, or scouting. Aren't you old enough for scouts?"

Kelly busied himself with filling his plate and passing the food. How did you make your father learn that you didn't like ball games? It seemed like the whole world thought you were crazy if you didn't like to play ball.

"Dad, I'm no good at stuff like that." Whew! He'd said it.

"No good?" Dad spoke loudly and with a wide smile.

Kelly wondered what inside feelings Dad was covering. Feelings of wishing he had a boy who was good at ball, probably.

"And you never will be good until you try, will you, sport?"

"Speaking of trying," Mother said. Kelly knew what was coming. He wanted to crawl under the table, crawl

into a hole like a fiddler crab, pull something over his head and stay until the tide had lowered. "Wasn't today the day for your progress report?"

Shannon gave him one of her unpleasant grins. Kelly swallowed. Usually you didn't hop up and down from the O'Brien dinner table. But Mother was holding out her hand and Kelly knew she meant for him to get up. He pushed away from the table and lumbered to his room. Flipping through his book, he thought for one happy moment he'd lost the dreaded paper. But when he held the covers and shook the book, it fell out. Going down the stairs, he felt he was going to his execution. They wouldn't actually chop his head off, but it might be even worse.

Mother looked at the paper, said "Oh, dear," quietly, and handed it to his father.

"Kelly, son." Mr. O'Brien shook his head sadly. "Son, we love you so much. We only want you to be satisfied with yourself, and we know you are not satisfied with this." Holding the report in one hand, Kelly's father tapped it into the palm of the other hand.

"Yes, sir," Kelly said, not meaning to agree but to fill the space when his father paused. Kelly knew perfectly well who wasn't satisfied.

"You're going to have to work really hard," Dad continued. "I think one thing you need, Kelly, is some restriction concerning the creek." There was the axe.

Kelly kept his eyes on the yellow flowers on his plate. More and more of them appeared as his food disappeared. If they wanted him to be satisfied with himself, and the creek satisfied him most, how would restrictions about the creek help him? He didn't understand. His parents volleyed words across the table.

"Until he shows some definite improvement in school," Mother said. "We know you love the creek. So you will work hard to keep your privileges. Right, Kelly?"

"Yes, ma'am," he mumbled. He was in a vise, being squeezed between his creek and not being smart, like Shannon, or good in sports, like Zack. Didn't they know he was smart in the creek? Unfortunately for him, "creek" wasn't on his progress report.

"And I'd like a daily progress report," Mother said. Kelly groaned. "I'll talk to Mrs. Jordan about sending me a note everyday. And now, about this man in the marsh," she said, changing the subject at last. "You know we don't like you talking with strangers."

Phillip, a stranger? Kelly thought. Weren't they going to leave him anything good?

"Don't you know he could kidnap you?" Shannon said, gloating, making grasping motions with her hands. "Drag you away through the marsh and we'd never see you again?"

"What a relief," Kelly said.

"It's not funny," Mother scolded.

"Phillip is not a stranger, Mom." Kelly put down his fork. "He goes to Brunswick Junior College and he is doing a biotic study in the marsh." He thought the word "biotic" would impress them, but they only waited for him to say more. He swallowed. He should have told them about Phillip before. He had kept Phillip private, his own personal treasure.

"He's studying marine biology," Kelly said, laughing and trying to keep the conversation from being so serious. "When he first told me, I thought he meant Marines—you know, like Army and Navy. I asked him where his uniform was."

Mother and Dad smiled. Shannon said, "Kelly, you're so dumb."

"What would you have thought if someone said 'marine'?" he challenged.

"I happen to know that the word 'marine' refers to things of the sea," she said loftily. "Besides, they wouldn't have him in the other Marines; he looks awful. Wild bushy hair and—"

"Go on, Kelly," Dad said, interrupting Shannon. "Tell us about this man, this college student. I must say"—Dad was looking across the table at Mother again—"I don't like the sound of it, his talking with strangers and lying about what he's been doing."

"For crying out loud," Kelly said in protest. He'd

only said he was playing football because he thought it would make his father happy.

"Is this the kind of behavior you learn from your, ah, friend?" Mother asked.

Kelly looked up in surprise. "For crying out loud," he said again. "You act like I never said 'for crying out loud' before!"

"That's enough, Kelly," Dad said.

Kelly stopped for a moment and looked at them. They were the adults and they could always win. He sighed and dropped his head.

"Yes, sir," he said quietly. He picked up his fork and resumed eating.

In his room after supper, Mother, like the teacher, handed him the templates. They were pieces of heavy cardboard with shapes cut out of them. There were circles and squares and triangles.

"We'll do at least five sets," Mother said. Kelly groaned and stretched the corners of his mouth, tightening his neck muscles at the same time.

"Kelly, please don't do that," Mother said.

He took the circle in his left hand and began tracing the shape with his right finger. A set was doing each shape ten times. He couldn't stand to think about doing five sets. The templates were a bright red-orange. Did someone suppose that their being colorful would make a person like them?

"Round," he said as he traced the circle, making his mouth round. "Try to make the sound round," he said, mimicking his teacher. That was silly; he couldn't make his mouth a square, or a triangle. After ten times around he put down the circle and picked up the square. When he tried to draw these shapes with his pencil, they came out all cockeyed. The exercises were supposed to train his hands to work with his brain. He'd been doing them for two months and he still couldn't draw a good round circle or a square with sharp corners.

"Bump, bump, bump, bump," he said, crashing his finger into each corner of the square frame. Then he bump, bump, bumped the triangle. As soon as he finished ten times around the triangle, his mother handed him the circle again.

"Oh, Mom," he complained.

"Come on, now, Kelly," she urged. "We knew this wasn't going to be easy. You have to keep working at it. It's like chipping through an iceberg. It's a lot of work, but if you keep at it, you'll get through."

"But it isn't doing any good," he cried. "I'll never get through!" She sat unmoving, and finally he began tracing around the circle again. "Round," he said, turning himself into a stone, a hard, unfeeling thing. "Round," he said dully as he continued around the circle. "Round."

Chapter Three

Kelly stood in class with his nose against the chalk-board. In each hand was a piece of chalk. His arms were moving up and around and down and around. He was marking lopsided circles on the chalkboard. It was one of the exercises he did in the special class he was in one hour every school day.

"Four, five, six . . . ," the others counted in a chant. In between the counting was laughter. The six of them took turns at the chalkboard, making the rounds ten times while the others counted. Why did they do everything by tens, he wondered? Ten was not the only number in the world.

"Ten," the class announced. He put down the chalk and stood back to look at what he had drawn. Just as he had told his mother last night, these exercises were not helping. The circles were still not circles and he was not improving. If he didn't improve, he would be kept from his creek. Zack was right, he was hopeless.

He sagged into the seat of his desk. Before he was settled Mrs. Jordan handed him the templates. Dutifully he traced the shapes with his finger.

"Bump, bump, bump," he said, tracing the points of the triangle. How could these exercises train his brain and his hands to work together? For a change, he went around each shape only nine times.

"Come on, now, Kelly," Mrs. Jordan said with excitement. She reached for his hand and pulled him to his feet. "You haven't walked the board yet." For her, because he liked her, he grinned. Inside, he sighed.

The board was a long two-by-four set on top of two concrete blocks. It was supposed to help train his brain and his feet to work together. Stepping onto the end, he wobbled his way along. Zack could plunk a board across the creek and run across like a squirrel. Kelly was sure that Phillip could, too. Anyone could. Anyone except Kelly.

"Wonderful, Kelly," Mrs. Jordan said. Her voice was sticky-sweet. What was so wonderful, Kelly wondered, about wobbling across a board? Sometimes he thought

Shannon was right. He was dumb. He was dumb in his mind and dumb in his body.

The doctor said it was his eyes. But if something was wrong with his eyes, why didn't he have glasses? He kept trying all the things they said, and it hadn't helped.

Back in regular class Kelly tried to sit still. Mrs. Jordan was his teacher here, too. There were the six of them from the special class plus a whole classroom more, including Zack. "If you can't do your work you can at least be still and quiet," they had told him. Boy, had they told him! Mother had told him. Father had told him, and Mrs. Jordan had told him. He'd been told, all right.

He squirmed in his desk. His arm swished across the top of the desk. "Be still," he said firmly to his arm. "You will get me in trouble." More trouble he certainly didn't want. Any more trouble and he would never get to go back to the creek. Dad had even threatened to have it filled in.

"Be still," Kelly told himself. Being still took every bit of his energy. Being still took every bit of his time. He forced himself to be still. He was as still as a stone.

"I wonder if Kelly can answer that question for us?" It was Mrs. Jordan, and she was talking to him. Kelly blinked. What question? He had been so busy being still he hadn't heard any question.

"Kelly?" She was looking at him, waiting for his answer. The whole class was looking at him. He knew she didn't mean to embarrass him. She had made an agreement with him to call on him only when she thought he knew the answer. Kelly blinked again. He rubbed his hands together and grinned.

"Well, I don't think Kelly can help us this time," she said. "But isn't Kelly behaving nicely today?" The class chattered. A whole sea of heads nodded toward Kelly. Kelly kept on grinning. Smash you all, he thought. Folding his arms across his chest, he stared into the corner. His eyes climbed to the ceiling.

The light was just right to show the silvery lines of a cobweb. Or was it a spider web? He looked carefully for a spider. Maybe it had gone to frighten Miss Muffet. Kelly's grin turned into a real smile. He could just see prissy Miss Muffet jumping up with a shriek.

What kind of spider lived in that web? Kelly wondered. One day he wanted to learn how to identify spiders by their webs. A spider web was the most fantastic design he knew. He loved to watch a spider spinning its web. There were a lot of things, he thought, that he learned by watching, like where fiddlers go when the tide comes in. Before the water was too high, fiddlers scurried into their holes and sealed them tight. In the hole was enough air to last until the tide went back down.

I am not dumb, Kelly thought to himself. I'm as smart as anybody in this room. He sat up straight and

held his chin high as he looked around the room. That's right, he thought, looking at Zack and his other classmates. Kelly O'Brien was as smart as any of them. What did it matter if they didn't know it?

"Who can tell us what gravity is?" Mrs. Jordan asked. Kelly heard the question this time. With his newfound sureness he raised his hand. He knew about gravity, Isaac Newton and the apple. Often, his mother read to him from the encyclopedia about things he wanted to know. He moved his tongue around inside his cheek.

"Kelly?" Mrs. Jordan called on him.

It was like blowing out a candle. Calling his name blew out his brain. He closed his hand to a fist and twisted his still-raised arm. The grin popped onto his face. He struggled, not only for the answer but for the question. What had she asked? Had he known the answer when she asked it? Or had he just thrown up his hand like a robot? He was doing so many things like a robot lately.

"Zack?" Mrs. Jordan gave up on Kelly. A titter of laughter went around the room. They all got laughs out of Kelly O'Brien. The grin stayed on his mouth but he felt all stiff inside. Zack answered the question smoothly.

Kelly stared at Zack. Zack used to be his friend, shoe and sock like Shannon and Nancy. When Kelly repeated first grade, they had been so happy to be in the same class. Even last year, when Kelly was eight and Zack was seven, Zack used to come play in the creek. Now all Zack wanted to do was play ball. If Zack couldn't kick something or throw something, Zack wasn't interested. Well, that was all right with Kelly. He didn't want Zack at the creek, anyway. The creek was his place to get away from people like Zack and Shannon and Mother and Dad. He pressed his arms close to himself, closing out the world. He pretended that he owned the creek himself. What more did he need? The thought got him through the day.

His mother had come with him this morning and explained to Mrs. Jordon about wanting a note every day. So, now, Mrs. Jordan gave him the note. She gave no hint of what it contained. As he left school he opened the note, wishing he could read it. If it said he had done well and tried hard he could go to the creek. He had tried. And Mrs. Jordan said "wonderful" when he crossed the board. But then, there were those questions he hadn't answered, and he'd had an awful time being still.

As he moved along he scuffed his shoes in the dirt. The dust swirled. His feet were galloping horses. Faster and faster the cowboy riders urged the horses. No. There were no cowboy riders. There were no riders at all. His feet were wild, free stallions. He lifted his head and whinnied.

"You're a funny boy, Kelly." It was Zack. Kelly barely heard the voice.

"I'm a stallion," Kelly said. He shook his head, letting his mane fly in the breeze. "You can be one, too." Kelly pawed the ground and quivered his nose.

"My stallion can beat yours," Zack said. Zack stirred the dirt and galloped away. Zack's stallion had two big wheels. For a moment Kelly pretended it was like it used to be. He galloped along behind Zack. But Zack didn't look back. Zack wasn't playing. Zack's wheels left Kelly's stallion feet far behind. Kelly couldn't ride a wheeled stallion; he couldn't keep his balance. Kelly galloped up to his house. He smacked the stallion on the rump and watched it run free. Leaping up the three front steps he fell, splat.

"Did you have a good day?" his mother asked as she met him at the door.

"Yup, until just this minute," he said, grinning and picking himself up. "Here's the note." He brushed past her and went into the kitchen. He lifted the lid to the cookie jar. Empty. Opening a cabinet he reached for the crackers.

"Mrs. Jordan doesn't say you had a good day," she said, following him into the kitchen as she read the note. He stuffed two crackers into his mouth. It was a mistake. Her announcement that it wasn't a good note had dried his saliva glands. The crackers soaked up all the moisture in his body. He moved his mouth, chewing, mashing. The crackers stuck all inside his mouth.

"You're still not trying, Kelly," Mother said. "Mrs. Jordan says it's your attitude." He leaned over the trash can and sputtered crackers out of his mouth. Not trying? How did they measure trying?

"Kelly!" Mother said sternly as he spit crumbs.

His guts were twisted with trying. Grabbing a glass, he splashed it full of water. He gulped mouthfuls and cleaned his mouth with his tongue.

"I *am* trying, Mom," he said. He put the grin on his face and, crossing his arms over his chest, folded himself up. "I try all the time. Honest."

"Now, Kelly. If you were really trying your teacher would know it. She's a very fine teacher."

"Maybe she just doesn't like me." It was the first thing that came into his head to say. He knew Mrs. Jordan did like him, and he liked her. But why did she write a note saying he wasn't trying?

"You have to believe in yourself, Kelly," Mother said.

"Sure, I believe in myself," he said. "I know I'm here." Clowning, he pinched himself and hollered to prove he was real.

"If you worked the templates for Mrs. Jordan like you did for me last night, I can see why she would say you didn't have the right attitude." He pictured himself tracing the shapes like a zombie. Was that a wrong attitude?

"What's an attitude?" he asked.

"It's the way you think or feel about something."

"Uh-oh," he said. In that case he knew he did have a bad attitude about those exercises. And ball-playing. Did he have any good attitudes? he wondered. Sure.

"Like I have a good attitude about the creek?" he asked. And Phillip, he thought, but since she considered Phillip a stranger he didn't say it.

"Yes," she said, mussing his hair with her hand. "You certainly do have a good attitude about the creek."

"Speaking of the creek," he began in what he thought was a cheerful manner. Immediately the comforting hand left his head and a stern look came onto her face.

"No more creek until your teacher feels that you are trying," she said firmly. "No more creek until you show a *lot* of improvement." There it was again, improvement. He guessed he'd never be able to go to the creek again.

"Yes, ma'am," Kelly said sadly. His voice was in the bottom of a pit with the rest of him. Could he help it if he couldn't do everything? Could he help it if he had a visual perception problem? He didn't ask for it. He didn't give it to himself. It was nothing he wanted.

He flipped the television switch and plunked down into a chair. He huddled himself like a bear in hibernation.

Chapter Four

Even though he couldn't see it from the chair, the creek pulled him like a magnet. He moved to the kitchen and looked out the window. Still, he couldn't see the creek. It was tucked under the bluff between the green of his yard and the gold of the marsh. He couldn't see Big Marshy, either, but he could see where it was. The marsh right next to the creek stayed green all year. Big Marshy was hiding beneath that pale green ribbon.

The marsh went on forever. Several miles away, the bridges to the offshore islands rose like towers from the marsh. The dark green islands were humps, like giant turtles in the gold marsh sea. The whole wonder of it called to him.

Without knowing it he pushed the door open. He stood there gazing and wishing. Suddenly he realized the door was open. He let it bang shut quickly. Mother came running.

"Oh," she said. "I thought you had gone out. Surely you have more sense than that." She turned and left the room. In a minute, Kelly kicked the door with his foot and let it bang again. She came again. Without a word, she reached over his shoulder and hooked the latch. That was easy enough. He unhooked the latch and swung the door again.

"Kelly O'Brien, you stop that!" She poked her head around the corner and scowled. Once again he shoved the door. This time she didn't look and she didn't say anything. He twisted his mouth from one side to the other. He sucked his bottom lip under his top teeth.

Once more he swung the door open. This time he slipped out. He pressed himself against the side of the house. He stood very still, not stone still but tiger still. He was alert and listening. He waited for the booming crash of her voice. It didn't come.

With a commando dash he ran, streaking across the grass toward the marsh. Taking the bluff with a leap and a slide, he disappeared over the edge. Checking, he peeked back over the rim. All clear. He rolled to his back and let out a huge sigh, then slid down to his boat.

The copper-gold marsh rose up about him and held him. The tide lapped at the marsh like a kitten lapping milk. The fiddlers, with their funny eyes, were staring. Kelly stared back. The tiny creatures moved along stuffing mud into their mouths. They ate what was good out of the mud, the way a fish did with water. Then the mud came back out, making tiny droodle humps across the bank. The crab tracks looked like squiggly roads and rivers on a mud map.

At school Kelly couldn't sit still, but he could be still at the creek. He liked to sit quietly, watching the crabs or looking for the herons or egrets or red-winged blackbirds. From somewhere within the marsh a marsh hen cackled. He heard one often, but seldom saw one. Marsh hens were shy birds and very good at hiding. Possums and coons he seldom saw, either, because they were nighttime creatures. But at low tide in the mornings he sometimes saw their tracks.

Noiselessly Kelly paddled down the narrow strip of water. The sun baked down on the top of his head and onto his bare arms. Though it was still winter, it seemed he could see the freckles popping out on his arm. The tide was coming in quickly, and the fiddlers were hurrying to their holes.

At the end of the runlet, Kelly stopped and cleared the fence of marsh grass. Maybe it wouldn't be much longer before Dad would have a boat; then they could go onto Big Marshy. Once, from this very spot, Kelly had seen porpoises humping along in Big Marshy. He wanted to open the gate and give them a chance to come into this little runlet and be his special friends.

He longed to call Phillip and hear the answering "Ho," but he didn't dare. Shannon might be around somewhere, and she was sure to know that he wasn't supposed to be here. She seemed to know everything about what he was and wasn't supposed to do.

A metal-rimmed ice-cream container had washed into the marsh near the fence. It was the kind they dipped from at the ice-cream store. Kelly had one in his bedroom for a trash can. He had painted it and decorated it himself.

This one in the marsh yawned roundly. With the paddle he fished the tub toward him. It reminded him of the circles he traced on the templates. A perfect round "O." He put his hand inside the rim and felt the shape. Around and around he moved his arm.

"I must believe this is going to help me," he said to himself, not believing it. "Round," he said aloud.

"Round," said a voice that was not Kelly's. Kelly jumped and looked up. There was Phillip, in his own boat, just on the other side of the gate. Phillip was mov-

ing one arm in a large circular motion and repeating "Round."

"Hey, Phillip," Kelly said, making his voice rush over his embarrassment. "I was looking for you." He pitched the ice-cream tub overboard, and it landed with a plop in the mud.

"And here I am," Phillip said. "What were you doing?"

"Just waiting around for you," Kelly said, careful to keep his eyes off the tub. Usually he picked up trash from the creek or marsh. Phillip must think it very strange for him to throw something down like that.

"No, I mean what were you doing with that?" Phillip stretched a scrawny arm toward the ice-cream carton. Kelly wanted to grin and tell Phillip he was just playing, but the grin and the words wouldn't come. He could never be fakey with Phillip. He shrugged.

"It's exercises," he said, feeling totally exposed in his stupidity. "Exercises for *dumb* people. For my hands, my eyes, my brain. I'm dumb, Phillip," Kelly shouted. "I'm dumb all over."

"Hey, come here, kid," Phillip called. Kelly didn't move. The one place he felt smart, knew he was smart, was in this creek and with Phillip. Now that was ruined, and because of those dumb exercises.

"Kelly!" Mother screaming his name was like a shot in the back. He had forgotten that he and Phillip were in the world. He had forgotten that he had slipped away without permission. For once he was glad to be called away from the creek.

"I have to go," he mumbled to Phillip. At least his family would be happy now. He would stay away from the creek. He couldn't risk being dumb around Phillip. The gate swayed as he pushed off with the paddle. Phillip put out a hand to steady it. Dad wouldn't have to fix it now. It didn't matter any more.

Rowing back to the hitching post was easy because the tide pushed him. Before he was up the bluff Mother reached down and grabbed him. She dragged him up the bank and started the spanking.

"Not only in the creek," she said between swings, "but talking to that stranger. He looks even worse than Shannon said." Kelly glanced back toward the gate. There was Phillip standing there watching. His mother's walloping hand behind him, Kelly stumbled all the way to the house. Every lick somehow offset his misery. Even when she plunked him in the tub and bathed him like a baby, he didn't protest.

"I'm not trusting you out of my sight," she said. She did, though. When he was clean she shoved him into his room and closed the door. "Don't you dare come out until I say so," she said. He couldn't remember ever having seen her so angry.

He sat on his bed staring at the door. As he stared,

he began to match her anger. If he knew how to do spells he would black-magic her. She didn't seem like the same person who rubbed his head or read to him from the encyclopedia. Could he help it that he didn't improve? Was it his fault that letters looked different from one time to the next? The "d's" and "p's" kept turning up-side-down and backward. Could he help that?

Stupid circles, anyway. He walked over and kicked a dent in the rim of his trash can. Circles and squares and walking on boards. What did they have to do with any-thing? He had a problem with his eyes that glasses wouldn't help, they said. An eye-to-hand problem, they said. They said. They said. What about what he said?

Picking up the trash can, he rubbed his hand around inside the rim. It was lopsided, now, like the circles he drew. His hand didn't travel smoothly around the rim. It bumped across the bent part. Kelly turned the tub upside-down. He rubbed the bottom part that wasn't bent.

"Round," he said slowly. He made his mouth round with the word. "Round," he repeated as his hand moved around and around. He smiled. He was beginning to feel the roundness. Putting the trash can down, he sat at his desk and drew circles with a pencil. He smiled to himself. He was really beginning to learn it. His circles looked full and fat, not lumpy and bumpy.

Pulling a drawer all the way out of his desk, he moved his hand along the inside edges. Bump at the corner, bump, bump, bump. His hand stayed on the edge all the way. With the pencil he drew a square. Usually he couldn't make sharp corners. No matter how hard he tried the corners usually rounded or slanted off. He "bumped" the pencil into an imaginary corner and changed directions. Bump, bump, and bump.

"Look at that beautiful square!" he exclaimed to himself. He forgot why he was in his room. He had to share his joy. Snatching up the paper, he ran out the door shouting.

"Kelly," his mother called to him in a warning voice.

"But Mom, look!" He bounded down the stairs.

"But look, nothing," she said, coming around the corner. She whirled him around and smacked him hard. Bump on the tail, he thought. Bump up the stairs.

"Yow!" he howled loudly when he slammed the bedroom door. He slapped the paper down on his desk top and threw himself onto the bed. It bounced him and he bounced back. He stayed there bouncing and glaring at the door.

After a while he opened the door quickly and put his paper on the hall floor by his door. A while after that he heard footsteps. They stopped.

"Kel, come look at this," his mother called to his

father. In a minute they were in his room hugging him and rubbing his hair and patting his back like he'd scored sixteen touchdowns. That, he guessed, was improvement.

Chapter Five

At school he could hardly wait to show Mrs. Jordan. Doing templates, he was an alive person instead of a robot. Shapes of circles, squares, and triangles went through his finger to his brain.

At the chalkboard he drew lopsided, but real, circles. The group still laughed as they counted, but they cheered, too. A grin came up from inside him. It was different, he knew, from one he forced onto his mouth. Walking the board, holding his arms out for balance, he was less tottery than usual.

"What do templates have to do with my feet?" he asked.

"Well, suppose I take this string," Mrs. Jordan said, taking a string from her desk. Holding one end of the string, she shook it. "See? I can move the whole string by shaking one end of it. But if I cut the string in only one place it affects the whole string, doesn't it?" With scissors, she made one cut and part of the string fell to the floor. Shaking the string, only the part still in her hand moved. The string on the floor was still.

"Yes, ma'am," he said. "But I still don't understand. Why are my feet better at crossing the board because my hands have learned the shapes?"

"You are just like this string," Mrs. Jordan said. "Your feet won't move if they are separated from the rest of you. Every part of you is connected with every other part."

"Oh," Kelly said happily. "You mean everything helps everything else?"

In regular class he was ready to try the alphabet. Just like he'd been told so many times, the letters were only circles and lines. What was so hard about circles and lines? On his tablet paper he began copying the letters from the chart above the chalkboard. A full round circle with a straight line touching its right side was a small "a," and "b" was a circle with a tall line starting above and coming down beside the left side. Part of a circle was "c."

By the time he got to "d" his hand was tired. The line came down on the wrong side of the circle. It looked just like the "b." He erased it. In writing the letter again, he made the very same mistake. This time as he erased he rubbed a hole in the paper.

He felt hot, as though everyone was watching him. Covering the paper with his arm, he looked around the room. Everyone was busy writing, writing quickly and easily, copying off the chalkboard. No one was paying any attention to him.

"May I help you with something, Kelly?" He jerked as Mrs. Jordan surprised him from behind.

"No, ma'am," he said. Smiling, he tried to capture some of the good feelings of a few minutes ago.

"Let me see your work," Mrs. Jordan said. Kelly kept on grinning, shook his head, and carefully kept his arm across his paper. A short time ago she had been so proud of him. He didn't want her to see that he still could not write his letters.

"Why don't you play the shape game?" Mrs. Jordan suggested. "Draw pictures of what you see. Do you see anything square?"

"The window," he answered dutifully. Folding over his messy paper, he drew a window. The sooner he began, the sooner she would walk on to someone else. It was discouraging to know that he was not improving after all.

"That's the nicest window you've ever drawn," she said.

Looking at what he had drawn, Kelly saw that all four corners met. "To tell the truth," he said, "it is." As Mrs. Jordan walked away he drew more details onto his window. Using narrow double lines, he marked off the windowpanes. A window, however, was not the letter "d." If he drew a window backward, it was still a window. The letter "d" backward was no longer a "d."

The word window has a "d" in it, he thought. Listening for the sounds, he said "window" softly to himself. How did you write it? To Kelly, it sounded like the wind with an "oh" at the end. With his pencil he drew streams of wind across his paper. At the end of the wind he drew a fat, round "O."

Maybe he could start his own kind of writing. Looking around the room he said words to himself. Desk. Floor. Door. None of those words worked for his new drawing-writing. Chalkboard. He grinned. He drew a board, reached under his desk for his crayons, and colored it white. A chalkboard. He smiled to himself.

At home his mother sent him to his room.

"Now that you are doing so well, you need to practice even more," she said. Ignoring his protests, she followed him to his room and started him on the templates. As soon as she was gone, he stopped. He didn't need circles and squares and triangles. What he needed was "d's" and "b's" and "p's."

He crawled across the bed and looked out at the creek. Face against the window, he felt the cool glass on his forehead and his nose. He pressed his tongue

against the cool smoothness and breathed fog on the pane. Without even knowing it, he rolled over and went to sleep.

Suddenly he awoke, banging his head against the windowsill. Holding his head, he muffled a howl. His heart was pounding. He looked around the room quickly. What had awakened him with such a jolt?

Below him came the sound of a deep, scratchy voice. Phillip? Was it Phillip? He pressed himself to the window but could see no one. The voice continued, stopping now and then, as in conversation. It was Phillip, he was sure. Phillip was at this house. Quietly, Kelly got up and tiptoed to the door. What was Phillip doing here? What was Phillip telling his mother? Opening the door, he sneaked down the stairs. Mother almost bumped into him as she came around the corner.

"Oh," she said in surprise. "Your friend Phillip is here to see you." She went back to the kitchen. "He was just coming down," Kelly heard her say to Phillip. Then she called, "Kelly, where are you?"

Kelly wrinkled and stretched his face. Seeing Phillip now, now that Phillip knew he was dumb, would spoil the whole memory of the friendship. Still, whatever Phillip had been saying to his mother had advanced Phillip from a stranger to a friend. Carefully, he peeked around the corner. Phillip happened to be looking at the exact spot where Kelly's head appeared.

"Ho, kid," Phillip called across the kitchen. "I brought my notebook to show you." Phillip waved the notebook above Mrs. O'Brien's head. His scrawny, hairy arms and legs stuck out from his faded marsh clothes. Curly hair and beard surrounded his head.

Slowly, Kelly crossed the kitchen toward his mother and Phillip.

"Mom, this is Phillip," he said, not knowing what else to say.

"I know," she said.

"I also came to see if everything was okay," Phillip said. "Any day you are not at the creek something must be wrong."

Kelly's tongue traveled around inside his mouth trying to make words. What could he say that would make any sense? Phillip wouldn't want to spend time with him now, even if he could go to the creek.

"Phillip and I have been talking," Mother said. "He's helped me to understand some things."

"He has?" Kelly said, wondering what they had been talking about. He had never known his mother to be interested in the creek except to help him look up stuff.

"I told your mother that you should tell your class about the marsh," Phillip said.

"Huh?" Kelly said. Why should he tell about the marsh? Everyone knew all about the marsh. Marsh was all around Brunswick.

"About fiddlers, for instance," Phillip said.

Kelly shrugged and rolled his eyes. He really would feel stupid telling people about fiddlers. "Everybody knows about fiddlers," he said.

Phillip laughed. "Some people don't notice what's right in front of their noses. I'll bet not one of your classmates, for instance, knows about the blue spot."

"Well," Kelly said, hesitating and hunching a shoulder.

"You could show them." Phillip clapped him on the back. "Can he come with me now to gather his specimens? I'll leave my notebook here for you to look at later." Phillip spoke to both Mrs. O'Brien and Kelly. Kelly held his breath. Phillip does want to be friends, he thought with amazement. And he's rescuing me. He knows I need the creek. "Fifteen minutes," Phillip continued. "It won't take fifteen minutes."

"All right," Mrs. O'Brien said, "if Kelly really means to take them to school."

"Sure I do," Kelly said quickly. He might be dumb, but he was no dummy.

"Fifteen minutes, then," she said. Kelly whooped and leaped out the back door. He raced Phillip to the bluff and scurried over the edge.

"A jar," Kelly said. "I don't have anything to keep them in."

"You can use one of mine," Phillip said. Phillip had lots of jars down by his study area. With a scooping movement the young man snared two sand fiddlers and plopped them into Kelly's hand. "Hold them until we get a jar."

The male fiddler grabbed the inside of Kelly's little finger as he closed his hand on the crabs. It didn't hurt, really, if you were expecting it. It was just like being pinched.

Phillip, hairy legs pumping, galloped along the muddy bank to the marsh. A few steps into the marsh he stooped and came up with two marsh fiddlers.

"That was fast," Kelly said.

"We don't want you to be late," Phillip said, handing the two to Kelly. "Do you know what you have?"

"Sure I do," Kelly said. "Mud fiddlers and sand fiddlers, a male and female of each." He closed his hand on the new pair. They reached Phillip's study area and Phillip held out a jar. Kelly deposited his four squirming specimens into the glass cage. He added some dribbles of mud and sand. Together he and Phillip ran back along the bank. It was such a friendship feeling, running along with Phillip.

"Go get 'em, kid," Phillip said as Kelly scrambled up the bank.

Chapter Six

Mrs. Jordan was happy that Kelly had brought something to share with the class. He held the jar tightly as he walked to the front of the room.

"Aw, it's just fiddler crabs," someone said, groaning.

"It's two different kinds of fiddlers," Kelly began.

"There's just one kind of fiddler and that's a fiddler," someone said.

"There are mud fiddlers and sand fiddlers," Kelly said. "The scientific names are *Uca pugnax* and *Uca pugilator*."

"Huh?"

"Oh, sure, Kelly."

"Yeah, sure," Kelly said loudly. "The mud fiddler is *Uca pugnax* and the sand fiddler is *Uca pugilator*."

"Listen to Kelly!" Everyone looked at him. The fiddlers scratched at him through the glass.

"I have a male and female of each," he said. "See the big claw? Only the males have this big claw. They use it to defend themselves." Slowly, he walked around the room so everyone could see. "The waving motions they make in defense look like they are playing the fiddle. That's why they're called fiddlers. If the big claw breaks off, another regular-size claw grows back in its place. Then the other claw develops into a big one."

"Yeah, I bet," said one of the smart alecks. Kelly kept on talking.

"The males eat with the small front claw. The females use both front claws to eat. They take mud into their mouths like a fish takes water. They don't eat the

mud, but they eat things out of the mud. You know, tiny things like diatoms or young crustaceans. Then they spit out the mud into a claw and set it aside. That's what makes those funny little droodles you see wherever there are fiddlers."

Kelly hardly stopped to take a breath.

"The blue mud fiddler, the *Uca pugnax,* is darker than the sand fiddler, to match the mud. See the blue spot between the eyes?" Half the students left their desks and crowded around him, saying, "Let me see, let me see."

After more explanations, Kelly finally returned to his own desk. It seemed to him the classroom was the most quiet he had ever heard, except when the principal came to visit.

"Well, Kelly," Mrs. Jordan said. "That was quite an oration!" Kelly blinked.

"An oration is a talk. A speech," she explained. Why did she think he'd made a speech? he wondered. He hadn't made any speech; he had only told about fiddlers. He poked his tongue into his cheek and swished his arms across the desk.

"It was quite brilliant," Mrs. Jordan said.

Brilliant? Him? His face felt hot. What was so brilliant about knowing fiddlers? Anyone could do that. They were right there in the marsh for anyone to see. Brilliant? Him? He began to grin.

After school Zack zoomed up on his bike. "Hey, Kelly. How did you find out all that stuff about fiddler crabs?"

Kelly, walking home from school as usual, moved his books from one hand to the other. He was no better at riding bikes than he was at playing football. He didn't feel steady on two wheels.

"How did you learn about fiddlers?" Zack repeated. Zack swung a leg over the bicycle seat and walked along pushing the bike.

"I just spend a lot of time at the creek," Kelly said. "I know what I see, that's all."

"You sure didn't see those crazy names in the creek," Zack said.

"Oh, that. *Uca pugnax* and *Uca pugilator.* Phillip tells me things. And Mom reads to me out of the encyclopedia."

"Gosh, my mother never reads to me," Zack said. "Who's Phillip?"

Kelly felt a rush of pleasure at telling Zack about Phillip. "He's a college friend of mine," Kelly said, feeling important. "He has a biotic study in the marsh."

"What are those names again?" Zack didn't seem impressed about Phillip. Kelly repeated the names.

"I can't even say them," Zack said. "What do they mean?"

Kelly hunched his shoulders. "Mom says that

scientists give Latin names to things. The 'pug' part means something about fighting. I don't remember the rest."

Zack's eyes widened. "Latin! That's another language, isn't it? Like Spanish or French? I don't even know *any* Latin." Kelly grinned. He didn't know any Latin, either, but if Zack wanted to think he did it was okay.

"Are you going down there this afternoon? To the creek?"

"Sure," Kelly said, fingering the note in his pocket. "I go there every day." It was a good note, he was sure. He only hoped the note would be enough to overcome his mother's anger. She was still mad at him for sneaking out the other day.

"Could I go with you? Please? I'll do everything you say."

Kelly looked sideways at Zack. Was this really Zack, asking to do something with Kelly? Was Zack really wanting to do something besides play ball?

"I never paid much attention to the fiddlers before," Zack said. Zack patted the back fender of his bicycle and Kelly hopped on. He carefully held his feet away from the spokes. Zack pedaled fast as they whizzed down the woodsy street toward home. When they came in sight of his house, Kelly tugged at Zack's shirttail.

"Let me off here," Kelly said. "Mom doesn't like me

riding double." Zack braked and put one foot down on the street.

"Mine, either," Zack grumbled. "Mothers won't let you do anything."

Kelly touched the pocket where the note was. He was hoping his mother would let him do one thing. If she let him go to the creek, maybe he and Zack could be friends again.

"I'll meet you at your house in just a minute," Zack said, riding away. Kelly ran home.

"Mom, Mom," he yelled as he came in the doorway. "I have a good note, I know I do." He waved it like a victory flag, holding his breath while she read it.

"I should say so," she said, smiling. Scooping her arm around him, she hugged him off balance. "Mrs. Jordan says you took part in class and knew more than anyone, even the teacher. She says you were brilliant."

"Wow!" Kelly shouted. He clasped his hands above his head and leaped. "Mom, can I—can I, please? It's improvement, isn't it?" He pulled his lower lip into his mouth. "It's really for Zack. Zack wants to learn more about fiddlers. That's what I was brilliant about."

She hesitated. Kelly nodded his head, trying to hypnotize her into nodding hers. The promise of good school days forever was in his eyes.

"I was so angry with you for sneaking out the other day," she said. "But that was the other day. This is today. Because of today, you may go." He circled her waist with his arms and twirled her around.

"You are the best mother in the whole wide universe!" His grin almost stretched right off his face.

"It doesn't mean, however, that you can leave your books on the floor." He didn't even remember putting them there. Snatching them up, he ran up the stairs two at a time without falling. He skidded back down just as Zack came.

61

Chapter Seven

The two boys ran across the backyard and slid over the edge of the bluff. Their pants gathered mud as they slid.

"Yuck," Kelly said happily. In reflex he dusted his pants. "Uck-yuck," he said, looking at his muddy hands. He waggled them in the water to rinse them.

"Tide's coming in," he said to Zack. "We'll have to catch the fiddlers before they run for their holes."

"Will we need your boat?"

"Sure," Kelly said, laughing. "I always need my boat, even if I don't need my boat." Running to the boat, he tossed Zack a life jacket from the seat compartment.

"First, I want you to meet Phillip," Kelly said, paddling toward the gate. "We can look for fiddlers and see Phillip at the same time." Stepping from the boat, he looped the rope around the end of the gatepost.

"Phillip," he called, cupping his hands around his mouth.

"Ho," Phillip called back.

"Ooshy-gooshy," Zack said. "Won't we get stuck?" Kelly looked over his shoulder at Zack, laughing. Being in the marsh with a friend made him feel shiny inside.

"Just follow me," he said, leading the way into the edge of the marsh. The grasses rose above their heads.

"Won't we get stuck?" Zack repeated. Kelly frowned. As often as Zack had been at the creek, he should know about getting stuck. How could someone live at the edge of the marsh and not know all about it? What Phillip said was true, Kelly thought, about some people not noticing things.

"Back there, maybe," Kelly said, pointing toward the creek, "but not here. The marsh roots grow so close together it's almost like a woven mat. It feels like walking on wet sponges." As they walked, he parted the grasses with his hands.

"Very well explained," said Phillip, coming toward them through the marsh.

"Oh, hey, Phillip," Kelly said happily. Now he was with two friends in the marsh. "Phillip, this is Zack. Zack, this is Phillip." He waved his arms in introduction. Phillip reached out and shook Zack's hand.

"Welcome aboard," Phillip said.

"Zack wants to see if he can tell the fiddlers apart," Kelly explained. Fast as anything, Phillip leaned down and scooped a fiddler from the floor of the marsh.

"What kind is it?" Phillip asked, putting the squirming creature into Zack's palm. The fiddler promptly pinched and Zack hollered, "Yikes!"

"Here, give him to me." Kelly held out his hand and Zack gave him the tiny attacker. Kelly let the fiddler grab hold of his finger.

"I see the blue spot!" Zack said. The bright spot was about the size of a pencil point. "It's a — a — "

"Blue mud fiddler," Kelly said, helping Zack remember. "Remember what I called the spot?"

"His life spot," Zack said proudly. "You said it disappears when they die. Does it really?" He looked at Phillip.

"It sure does," Phillip said.

"It's a male, too," Zack said happily. "Look at that big claw. I don't know if I believe that about its growing back, though."

"You can believe that, too," Phillip said.

"Phillip studies them," Kelly said. "For college." Maybe Zack hadn't heard him before when he'd said Phillip was in college.

"This is a neat place to play spies," Zack said, look-

ing all around. Phillip winked at Kelly. Phillip and Kelly didn't need to play made-up games at the creek. Just being there was enough.

"Hey, let's do it," Zack said.

"Do what?" asked Kelly. He'd already forgotten.

"Play spies," Zack said. "Let's go to that island part." Zack had already turned back toward the boat. What Zack called the "island part" was the section of marsh between Big Marshy and the curving runlet. Kelly looked at Zack's retreating back and then at Phillip. He wanted to stay with Phillip, but he also wanted to be friends with Zack.

"Phillip?" Kelly said, feeling stretched between his two friends.

"Hey, listen, kid. You run along and play with Zack and I'll see you later when I come to get my notebook, okay?" Phillip understood. And the way Phillip called him "kid" didn't make him feel like a kid at all. "I'm glad to have met you, Zack," Phillip called after Zack. Kelly smiled at Phillip and mushed his way through the marsh to the boat. He unhooked the rope and began rowing.

"Let me row," Zack said, almost commanding. Kelly looked up in surprise. No one had ever rowed this boat but Kelly O'Brien. Dad hadn't and Phillip hadn't. But friends had to share, didn't they? Captains did need mates. He pushed the oars toward Zack.

Zack was not good at rowing. The boat slushed into the marshy bank. Kelly wanted to take over. Instead, he made himself remember his own first attempts at rowing. The memory made him laugh. In response Zack laughed, and, laughing, they zigzagged their way down the creek.

Opposite the hitching post Kelly poled the boat into the edge of the marsh. There was a long board laying a pathway into the marsh. Around this, Kelly looped the boat rope. Then, as spies, he and Zack tiptoed along the board.

They hadn't gone far when Kelly stopped suddenly.

"Shh," he said. "A marsh hen, see?" Kelly stooped so Zack could look over his head. There ahead of them was a marsh hen, a clapper rail. She was strutting and poking her beak into the mud. She was probably eating mud fiddlers. They must feel scratchy going down, Kelly thought.

She moved jerkily, step, step, peck, peck. Yet as she moved she didn't stir a single stem of marsh grass. She wove herself in and out between the stalks. Kelly looked back. The grasses were parted, showing the way he and Zack had come. He and Zack were not natural creatures of the marsh. They were too big to walk without disturbing the grasses.

"What's so special about a marsh hen?" Zack complained. At Zack's voice the bird stepped faster. She

kept her head down and didn't look at the boys. In a
moment she had disappeared.

Kelly turned and frowned at Zack. "What's so special about a marsh hen?" he mocked. "What's so special about a fiddler crab? What's so special about you and
me?"

"Golly, Kelly, you don't have to get mad."

"You'll see a lot more fiddlers than you will marsh
hens, that's what," Kelly said. "You'll see thousands of
fiddlers." Holding his hands near Zack's face, he wiggled
all his fingers to indicate thousands. Each one of those
thousands was special to him. But the marsh hen was
special, too. He had been waiting for the chance to watch
her, to study her. He wanted to know her as he did the
fiddlers.

"So, I'm sorry, I'm sorry," Zack said angrily. "You
can have your old marsh hen. Who wants it? You can
have your old smelly marsh and your dirty old creek, too.
You're dumb, anyway, Kelly. You can't even read."

Zack stomped his foot and the marsh splatted under it. Kelly stood speechless, watching while Zack stalked back to the creek. He watched Zack struggle with the board, lift it, and let it fall across the creek. Another splat. Kelly's voice was stuck in his throat. He was unable to make the sounds to call Zack back.

"Who cares about your old *Uca*-stupid-*pugnax,* anyway," Zack said. Picking up the boat rope, he scampered across the board and yanked the boat across behind him. Then he continued up the bank and disappeared.

Kelly walked to the creek, staring at his boat on the other side. The board Zack had crossed so easily might as well have been across the Grand Canyon. The water seemed threatening as it flowed under the board. Never seasick in his boat, he felt dizzy just thinking about crossing that board.

"I am an *Uca*-stupid Kelly," he thought. He couldn't read or write. He couldn't cross a simple board and he couldn't even keep a friend. How really stupid, he thought, to have to swim across the creek rather than cross on the board.

He clenched his fists and squinted his eyes. Then, almost as if he had been pushed, he charged onto the board and kept running. To his surprise, he landed on the mud bank near the hitching post. For a feeling of comfort and safety he hopped into his boat. Chin in hands, he sat slumped. His heart was beating wildly.

The tide lapped in and began creeping under the boat. Bits of marsh grass floated on the dark murky water. The last of the fiddlers scrambled for their holes. The gentle magic of the creek calmed him.

"I did it!" he shouted, and he pushed the boat into the water. A night heron swooped and circled and settled, disappearing into the marsh.

"I did it!" he shouted to the heron. He paddled slowly, silently, rowing toward the fence. "And I have my creek," he talked aloud to himself, "and my boat. And I do have a friend." His friend understood the importance of a marsh hen. His friend could also help him learn to read. He would learn. He was learning already, no matter what Zack said.

"Phillip," Kelly called. Nearing the fence, he called again. "Phillip." As he tied the boat to the fence, Kelly heard the answering "Ho."

🌿 Doris Buchanan Smith

is mother to five school-age children, four of her own and one for whom she and her husband are permanent guardians. The Smiths have also been parents to more than twenty-two foster children. Mrs. Smith's experiences have given her exceptional insight into the problems of being young as well as those of growing up. Now that her children are in school, she spends a minimum of three hours a day writing. She also likes animals and the woods, and is interested in nature and conservation. *A Taste of Blackberries*, her first book, won the Georgia Children's Book Award for 1974 and the 1973 Child Study Association Annual Award, and was named an A.L.A. Notable Children's Book for 1973.

🌿 Alan Tiegreen

spent his childhood in Idaho, Nebraska, and Alabama, graduated from high school in Ohio, and got his college degree in Mississippi and his graduate degree in California. He has now settled down in Georgia, where he is a professor of art at Georgia State University.

His paintings have been exhibited in numerous one-man shows throughout the United States and he has illustrated many children's books, but his interests aren't confined to art. He plays Dixieland jazz on both piano and banjo (though not at the same time), builds furniture, tinkers with mechanics, and plays tennis. Mr. Tiegreen is married and has three children.